D0987096

GEORGIE GRASSHOPPER'S EAR

SALLY'S GARDEN STORY

Library of Congress Cataloging in Publication Data

Rippon, Sally, 1967–
    Georgie Grasshopper's ear.

    (Sally's garden stories)
    Summary: Dennis Dormouse thinks Georgie is deaf, until he discovers that his ears are on his front legs, just below the knee.
    [1. Grasshoppers—Fiction. 2. Ear—Fiction] I. Title.
II. Series: Rippon, Sally, 1967–   . Sally's garden stories.
PZ7.R488Ge   1982   [E]   82-12237
ISBN 0-86592-792-8

Published by The Rourke Corporation, Inc., P.O. Box 711, Windermere, Florida 32786. Copyright © 1982 by The Rourke Corporation, Inc. Ally copyrights reserved. No part of this book may be reproduced in any form without written permission from the publisher. Printed in the United States of America.

74564

SALLY'S GARDEN STORY

GEORGIE GRASSHOPPER'S EAR

by Sally Rippon

Illustrated by Malcolm Walker

THE ROURKE CORPORATION INC.
Windermere, Florida   32786

Georgie Grasshopper sat on a blade of grass in the garden. He was watching Monty Mouse leap from bush to bush.

1/13/83 : 7/20/83 : 16 (6.10) American

Monty Mouse thought it was
fun to take such big leaps. He
would spread out his tail behind
him like a parachute.

"Look at me!" he cried to Georgie
as he took a flying leap onto the
grass. "Wasn't that clever?" he
asked.

Monty is quite a show-off.

Georgie decided he had had enough of Monty. He did not answer. He just sat and stared. He was pretending he had not heard a word.

"He must be deaf" thought Monty.

Of course, he never thought that Georgie might not want to answer. Show-offs always think that people are as interested in them as they are.

Monty ran to tell everyone that
Georgie Grasshopper was deaf.

The first person he met was
Tommy Tortoise. "Tommy, do you
know what?" asked Monty,
knocking on Tommy's shell.

"What?" asked Tommy, sticking his head out of his shell.

"Georgie Grasshopper is deaf!" he cried.

Tommy just grunted and put his head back in his shell.

So, Monty went on until he met Mary Ann Mouse.

"Mary Ann, do you know what?" asked Monty.

"What?" asked Mary Ann.

"Georgie Grasshopper is deaf!" he cried.

"Oh!" cried Mary Ann, "Let us go and tell Edward Owl."

Edward Owl lived in a big oak tree on the edge of Sally's garden. He was very wise and clever.

Quickly, they got to Edward Owl's oak tree. They told him that Georgie Grasshopper was deaf. Edward said, ''I would be very surprised if that were true. Somehow I do not think it is. Did you try speaking into his ear?''

''No,'' said Monty.

''Well, go and try then'' said Edward Owl.

So off went Monty and Mary Ann.
Soon they were both back. "He
does not have an ear!" cried Monty.

"No ear! Nonsense!" said Edward.
"You did not look in the right
place."

"Well, where should I look?"
asked Monty. "Aren't all ears in
the same place?"

"Of course not!" laughed Edward, "Come on, and I will show you where Georgie's ear is."

"I always thought that all insects had ears in the same place," said Monty thoughtfully.

They went to where Georgie stood. Edward Owl said, "Hello Georgie, how are you?"

"I am very well, thank you," answered Georgie politely.

"Good" said Edward. "Would you mind holding up one of your front legs?"

Georgie held out his leg and there was his ear just below his knee!

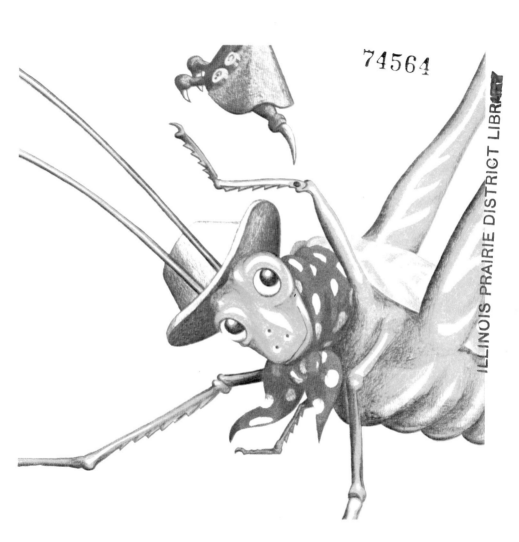

74564

"You see," said Edward Owl, "Georgie has ears on his front legs. His cousin the cricket has ears on his back legs. Some other members of their family have ears just below their tummies."

"What silly places to have ears!"
laughed Monty. Monty thought
everyone had to be like him.

"Why shouldn't they have ears on
their legs?" asked the wise old
owl.

Monty could not answer that one.

YOU ARE LIKE NO ONE
ELSE. YOU ARE ONE OF
A KIND!